All the King's Women

5 ONE ACT COMEDIES &
3 MONOLOGUES

by Luigi Jannuzzi

A SAMUEL FRENCH ACTING EDITION

SAMUEL
FRENCH
FOUNDED 1830

NEW YORK HOLLYWOOD LONDON TORONTO

SAMUELFRENCH.COM

ISBN 978-0-573-69666-4   Printed in U.S.A.   #29046

IMPORTANT BILLING AND CREDIT REQUIREMENTS

All producers of *ALL THE KING'S WOMEN must* give credit to the Author of the Play in all programs distributed in connection with performances of the Play, and in all instances in which the title of the Play appears for the purposes of advertising, publicizing or otherwise exploiting the Play and/or a production. The name of the Author *must* appear on a separate line on which no other name appears, immediately following the title and *must* appear in size of type not less than fifty percent of the size of the title type.

SET
Bare Stage

TIME
1946 – Today

ACT ONE

Scene:

INTERMISSION

ACT TWO

Scene:

PRODUCTION NOTES

Casting: Casting is extremely flexible. And since this play is 5 one act and 3 monologue comedies, there are many ways this play may be presented. It can be performed with as few as 3 females and 1 male or as many as 17 females and 1 male or many female/male variations between. Feel free to change genders for salespeople, secretaries, guards, etc.

Single Set: This is all that is needed. Set pieces should be kept to a minimum. The first production used only three black squares and minimum props. Rely on the audience and their imagination to bring the rest. They will reward you for that opportunity.

Costumes, Props and Projections: Costumes can be as simple as all wearing black and using suggested props. Projections can be used if you have the technology. A suggestion would be to show appropriate photos of the time period between scenes.See my website: www.LuigiJannuzzi.com for ideas.

Transitions and Music Use: Between scenes we used recorded radio addresses that include news from that date. Find them enclosed. If you can use music due to ASCAP sampling rule for High School, College, University and Community Theatre, (find link on my website) perhaps you can use both. (From NYTheatre.com:) "Transitions between scenes are not, as one would assume, with Elvis's music, but anchored by recorded radio addresses that reinforce the appropriate historical flavor of the current events of the times." Be creative!

Order of Scenes: I feel that this is the order that the show runs best. It ends in the present and it will be your perfect ending. Directing this play you will find that since this is divided into separate vignettes, the entire cast doesn't have to be there all the time, which is a lot easier on the cast and director.

Tone of the play: Warm, lively and fast. Please stay away from anger. There is none of that emotion written in this play. Anger is just not funny. Frustration is, but not anger. Yet amateur actors always go right for anger, which is the easiest emotion to act, and it ruins comedies all the time. Please show this paragraph to any who try. After playing anger, amateurs love to add curse words. Please do not allow that either. There are none in this play for a reason. It doesn't need any. It's a comedy.

Please go to my website and email me any comments, questions or pictures. I'd love to post them on my site to brag about your production and creativity. So if you are using a scene for forensics, a one act competition or in a collection of one acts, I'd love to hear how it went.

NOTE: *One Tupelo Saleswoman, The Censor and the King, When Nixon met Elvis, Warhol Explains Art to Elvis* and *One Private Guard* are all based on actual events in the life of Elvis Presley.

Links about Elvis, such as the Billboard Top Singles statistics by their years, are listed on my website: www.LuigiJannuzzi.com

Have fun. It was fun writing these plays. Audiences love them and applaud often.

Break a guitar string!

Note on cover: One guitar string is missing, the E string for Elvis.

SPECIAL THANKS

Alleen Hussung, the late William (Bill) Talbot, and all at Samuel French, Inc., Brandon Whitehead, co-producer., Ralph Sevush & David Faux at The Dramatist Guild, The Author's Guild, Nancy E. Wolff, Esq. at Cowan, DeBaets, Abrahams & Sheppard, LLP., Luis Angulo of La_Designs, Joe DeVito III, Weist-Barron Studios, 35 w 45 Street & Manager Charles F. Wagner IV, Roberta E. Zlokower: RobertaontheArts.com, Nancy Kim at NYTheatre.com, Pete Ernst & The Waterfront Ensemble/NJ Dramatists for supporting new works. Leecia Manning who directed the first reading at The DeBaun, Hoboken, NJ. Karen Greatti, Terri Campion, Jeff Baskin, Jeff Biehl, Lisa Rudin, Marcia Finn, Cynthia Granville, Michael Giorgio, Alice Connorton, Tim Barrett, Jennifer Kotrba, Judy Bard, David Tyson, David Walters, Joan Saporta, Michael Cleeff, Gabor & Susanne Barabas for presenting a reading of the plays at NJREP in Long Branch, NJ. Michael R. Duran, Arlene Schulman (directors) with Diana Devlin, Stacie Lee Lents, Brenton Popolizio, Cindy Carver and Alice Connorton. Mark Dunn and Joel Stone.

Brandon Whithead for directing and co-producing the Midtown International Festival production. The cast: Rebecca Bateman, Alisha Campbell, Craig Clary, Jennifer Blevins, Jessica Asch and Lloyd Fass for their great talents.

Mario Fratti for all his advice and confidence. Louis and Mark Jannuzzi for all their support.

The New Jersey State Council On The Arts, The National Endowment for the Humanities, The Geraldine R. Dodge Foundation, Helen Waren Mayer, & The Princeton University Library.

John Chatterton, Emileena Pedigo, Bob Ost, Glory Sims Bowen, Judd Hollander and the Midtown International Theatre Festival Staff.

Elvis Presley and his dedicated fans everywhere!

ABOUT THE AUTHOR

All The King's Women played to spectacular reviews at the Midtown International Festival in New York City and are Luigi Jannuzzi's twentieth to twenty-eighth published plays. You can find set ideas as well as reviews from the original production at Luigi's website: www.LuigiJannuzzi.com

The author's other published comedies include:

Full lengths: *Night of The Foolish Moon, For The Love of Juliet* and *Exhibit This! -The Museum Comedies.*

One Acts: *A Bench At The Edge, The Appointment, The Barbarians Are Coming,* and *With or Without You.*

Exhibit This! -The Museum Comedies, was the #1 Pick of *New York Magazine,* winner of the Perry Award for the best play in New Jersey Theater, played to tremendous reviews, awards and sold out performances in New York City. These 13 one acts won 3 Samuel French Off Off Broadway Short Play Festival Finalist Awards and two Off Off Broadway Awards (OOBR. com).

Luigi's play *A Bench At The Edge* won best one act in Ireland in 1999 and best one act in Scotland and The United Kingdom in 2001. He is a recipient of two New Jersey State Council on the Arts Fellowships, two Geraldine R. Dodge Grants, three National Endowments for the Humanities (2000 at Rutgers U., 1998 at Columbia U., and 1995 at The U Of Vermont) the 1986 Goshen Peace Prize, a 2000 and 1998 Finalist in the Eugene O'Neill National Playwriting conference, and is a 2007 - 2009 James Madison seminar participant at Princeton University.

He is a member of the Dramatist Guild, Author's Guild, NJTEC, NJ REP, the Metropolitan Theatre Company, and NJDramatist/Waterfront Ensemble. Mr. Jannuzzi born in Bound Brook, N J, educated at Raritan Valley Community College, received a B.A. from Salem College, W est Virgina, and a M.A. from the University of Notre Dame. He is a full-time Creative Writing and Drama teacher in New Jersey. For more information see *Contemporary Authors* & *Who's Who In America* online in your local library.

"The mind cannot absorb what the rear end cannot endure."
– Moliere

ACT I

INTRO TO SCENE ONE: "ONE TUPELO SALESWOMAN"

(Lights fade in theatre, and the following is heard:)

RADIO VOICE. Good Morning Mississippi. It is a chilly January 8th, 1946.

In World News, representatives from many nations have great hope for a new organization called The United Nations that is set to hold its first session in London in two more days.

In National News, a new invention called an Electronic Numerical Intergrator and Computer which takes up a room 30 feet by 50 feet at the University of Pennsylvania will begin calculations this week.

And President Truman today,...*(trailing off)*...will meet with Congress...

(Pause. Lights up on Scene One.)

ONE TUPELO SALESWOMAN

SET
Bare stage

TIME
January 8th, 1946

PLACE
Tupelo, Mississippi

CAST
Saleswoman

ONE TUPELO SALESWOMAN was first produced by the Metropolitan Theatre Company in New York City as a selection of the Midtown International Theatre Festival, at the Where Eagles Dare Theatre, 347 West 36th Street, on July 18, 2007. Executive producer, John Chatterton; managing director, Emileena Pedigo; artistic director, Glory Sims Bowen; marketing director, Bob Ost. The play was directed by Branan Whitehead; stage managed by Lloyd Fass; produced by Luigi Jannuzzi/ Branan Whitehead; lighting and sound design by Lloyd Fass and Branan Whitehead. The cast was as follows:

SALESWOMAN*................................JESSICA ASCH

*Also appeared as **SALESWOMAN**............JENNIFER BLEVINS

(Lights rise on **SALESWOMAN** *who is standing center stage.)*

SALESWOMAN. *(to offstage left)* Yes, Sir. Light bulbs? Aisle four, half way. You're welcome.

(to audience)

When I first saw the little boy enter this hardware store, I said to myself, "My God, there is something wrong with that child," which is a heck of a thing to say about a eleven year-old holding his Mother's hand, entering a hardware store. But that's what I felt.

(to offstage left)

Yes, Miss? Ax handles, 7th aisle, all the way down.

(to audience)

'Cause I had this odd feeling. And I remember thinking, "I don't want anything to do with this kid, I'm going to go to the bathroom, won't be my customer." I turned, a paper fell off a shelf, I stooped to pick it up... phone rang, my manager took it. The other salesman in the center, I heard his name being yelled from the back cause some rakes were falling. And when I came back up...the little boy, his mom and that odd feeling were standing right in front of me. *(to off right)* Sir? Candy is aisle one, boxed chocolates half way down, loose stuff in front of the register. You're welcome.

(to audience)

And the odd little boy's Mother says to me, "It's his Eleventh birthday, we're here for a present." So I say, "Isn't that wonderful, how old are you, son?" And the boy says, "Old enough for a 22 Rifle!" I look at the mother, and the mother's going like, *(shaking head no)* giving me the universal silent Mother sign for "over my dead body." So, like an idiot, I say, "So son, what would you like?" And, of course, the son says, "A 22 Rifle, please, with 6 cartridges boxes." The Mother is now staring at me, eyes buggin' out of her head, as if to say, "What is wrong with you woman, do you not understand the universal silent Mother sign for, 'No?'"

(to off right)

The bathroom? All the way back past the garden supplies. Women left, Men right.

(to Audience)

So I stoop, get down, right to the level of the boy's face barely reaching over the counter and I say, "Son, instead of a 22 rifle...how about if I show you...a brand new,... guitar?" Now...this child, this eleven year-old child, is looking at me with the same expression that a cow has when watching a train going by. You know what I'm talking about? You ever watch a cow watch a train go by? You know that "I don't know what it is... but I don't want any part of it" look? Well, that's what this kid's giving me.

(to off left)

Yes, Sir? Asbestos insulation? Aisle five, Plumbing.

(to audience)

So, of course, I say it again, "A guitar's wonderful. You can learn how to play and read music, be cultured, I took piano lessons and I have never regretted it." I now notice the mother is smiling, but the kid is giving me the silent, "No," thing. So I say, "How'd you like to just look at one of these guitars, huh?" Now the kids eyes are starting to swell up with tears. He looks up at his Mom and says, "Mom, you said." "But son," she comes back with, "They are just too dangerous." Then all hell broke loose. The kid started screaming. I mean this little boy had a temper tantrum, he fell on the floor. I took off to get the guitar.

(to off right)

What? No, your car is safe there. This is Tupelo. In fact, I'll keep an eye on it.

(to audience)

And I remember thinking to myself, "Whatever I do, I can't let this kid touch it, cause he's going to smash it, and I'm going to pay for it. Here it's payday, I'm getting my check in an hour, and the last thing I need is to have money deducted 'cause of this eleven year-old." So I come back, place the guitar on the countertop, and the mother is poking at him. You know that dagger of morality, index finger, poking that mother's do. And she's saying, "Son, take this now." And the kid's saying, "No." And she's saying, "This is it, or nothing." And the kid's taking these deep breaths, you can see his nostrils flaring. 'Cause the kid's thinking, "I don't want nothing, but I don't want this either." So then I hop in with my big sales line. I use this a lot cause everyone wants to be a country western singer. Especially around Tupelo, Mississippi cause everybody wants to be like Mississippi Slim. Who's a local boy, so famous and all. And I know this kid knows who Slim is, every kid his age is a fan. So I say, "You know who Mississippi Slim is, don't you?" The boy says, "Yes, Ma'am." And I said, "Well, you take this and learn how to play it, you may be famous someday like Mississippi Slim."

(to off right)

Yes, Miss? Harmonicas? Yes, right inside that glass case, if you see something you want, I'll get it out.

(to audience)

And it was just at that point that I could just see the defeat in this boy's face. The anger just right there. He was just looking at that guitar. And I just knew this guitar ain't going nowhere but a closet. But I pushed it, I pushed 'cause I knew his mother wanted me to push it. I said, "Son, what is your name?" "Elvis," the kid says. And I said, "Elvis, what's your last name?" "Presley," he adds. "Elvis Presley, I'm going to remember that name," I said, "'Cause someday I might hear about you and I'm going say that I was the lady who sold him his first guitar when he wanted a rifle." Of course, the kid's having nothing of the humor here. And the mother's nodding, "That's right you may be another Mississippi

Slim, Elvis." Elvis just standing there stunned. I took
the twelve dollars, ninety-five cents. The mother took
the guitar, tried to hand it to the little boy, he looked
down. I reached over the counter, gave him a bag
of pics, a tuning pipe, a handful of lollipops. Said,
"Happy eleventh birthday!" The little boy said, "Thank
you, Ma'am." Walked out.

(to off right)

Which Miss? The blue guitar? Twelve dollars, ninety-
five cents. Would you like to see it? I'll be right there.

(to audience)

But why I bring this up, is cause my mother would
always say she would get these odd feelings when she
was around something that was going to happen. And
I never knew what she was talking about till that little
boy walked into this hardware store. 'Cause I'm telling you...I have a very odd feeling about that little boy.
Like something's going to happen with that little boy.
And I fear, 'cause I don't know how to interpret these
feelings. And I hope I'm wrong. But I just pray that
that little boy doesn't do something really crazy someday...with a gun.

(as an afterthought...)

Or with that guitar.

(Lights fade. Blackout.)

INTRO TO SCENE TWO: "THE CENSOR AND THE KING"

(Lights fade in theatre, the following is heard:)

RADIO VOICE. In national news, President Eisenhower was released from Walter Reed Hospital following intestinal surgery, and will be traveling to recuperate at his home in Gettysburg, Pennsylvania.

In show news, Pulitzer Prize-winning dramatist Arthur Miller married film actress Marilyn Monroe in White Plains, New York. The service lasted less than five minutes. Mr. and Mrs. Miller then got into their sports car and disappeared into traffic.

And tonight on The Steve Allen Show, the new Elvis Presley will sing his controversial rock and roll hit song and also appear in a comedy sketch with Allen and guests Imogene Coca and Andy Griffith.

In sports, Casey Stengel and the league leading... *(trailing off)*...New York Yankees defeated

(Pause. Lights up on Scene Two.)

THE CENSOR AND THE KING

SET

Bare Stage with desk, 2 dog carriers & phone

TIME

June, 1956

PLACE

New York City

CAST

Abby

Barbara

Cynthia

*(Two Dogs bark at certain times, but are not seen.)

THE CENSOR AND THE KING was first produced by the Metropolitan Theatre Company in New York City as a selection of the Midtown International Theatre Festival, at the Where Eagles Dare Theatre, 347 West 36th Street, on July 18th 2007.Executive producer, John Chatterton; managing director, Emileena Pedigo; artistic director, Glory Sims Bowen; marketing director, Bob Ost. The play was directed by Branan Whitehead; stage managed by Lloyd Fass; produced by Luigi Jannuzzi/ Branan Whitehead; lighting and sound design by Lloyd Fass and Branan Whitehead. The cast was as follows:

ABBY . . . . REBECCA BATEMAN

BARBARA . . . . ALISHA CAMPBELL

CYNTHIA . . . . JESSICA ASCH

*Also appeared as **CYNTHIA**. . . . . JENNIFER BLEVINS

(Lights rise on bare stage with desk and chair. Upon desk is a phone and two large dog carriers. The dog carriers are facing away from the audience, and on the back of each is the sticker: "Live Animal." A tuxedo is draped over the chair.)

(**ABBY** *is on hard wired phone, pacing in front of desk.*)

ABBY. Steve…Mr. Allen, calm down, you're getting yourself bent out of shape about this. It's going to go fine.

(pause)

No, I am not taking this lightly. I think we have Presley over a barrel and he knows it.

(pause)

Steve…Steve? *(taking phone away from ear)*
Go on hang up. Great.

(Hangs up phone. **BARBARA** *enters.)*

BARBARA. He's coming down the hall.

ABBY. Great.

BARBARA. Do you think he's going to back out of all this?

ABBY. He can't.

BARBARA. And if they argue, do we negotiate?

ABBY. No! Mr. Allen does not want to negotiate. Presley wants to be on television, this is how he's going to do it. This is only a final meeting to pick up the tux and pick a dog.

BARBARA. *(to* **HOUND ONE***)* Hello. Woof, woof, woof, woof. Oh, they are cute.

ABBY. Aren't they?

BARBARA. *(to* **HOUND TWO***)* And so are you. You think one of them is going to stand still for this?

ABBY. Dogs love music.

(Knocks are heard.)

ABBY. Come in.

BARBARA. *(to* **HOUND ONE***)* Give me paw. Ohhhh.

(to **HOUND TWO***)* Give me paw. Ohhhhh.

CYNTHIA. *(from off)* Hi.

ABBY. Hello.

CYNTHIA. *(entering stage)* Hi.

ABBY. You are?

CYNTHIA. Cynthia, Colonel Tom Parker's secretary.

ABBY. I'm Abby. Steve Allen's secretary. Nice to meet you.

CYNTHIA. Same here.

ABBY. But where are Colonel Parker and Mr. Presley?

CYNTHIA. I'm here for both. And they have three questions and a request.

ABBY. Great. Oh, this is Barbara.

CYNTHIA. Hi.

BARBARA. Hello.

ABBY. Barbara is the secretary for our network censors. She'll be taking the minutes.

CYNTHIA. Nice to meet you.

BARBARA. Nice to meet you.

CYNTHIA. Oh…the Basset Hounds?

ABBY. Yes.

(**CYNTHIA** *over to carrier.*)

CYNTHIA. I love Basset Hounds. *(pause)* "Meow." *(Pause,* **CYNTHIA** *smiles.)* Look at those eyes. Hello. And hello to you too. *(pause)* This looks like a female.

ABBY. It is.

CYNTHIA. And this looks like a male.

ABBY. Female, too.

CYNTHIA. Two females. Elvis gets along best with them.

ABBY. I'll say. We're trying to pick one. So if you have any preference.

CYNTHIA. Lucky dogs.

ABBY. Now, very quickly, Cynthia. And I'm sure you received our memo on this.

CYNTHIA. We did.

ABBY. The Colonel and Mr. Presley are aware that there will be a Hound Dog on a pedestal?

CYNTHIA. They are.

ABBY. It's going to have a short leash so he can't move around. *(pause)* The hound dog that is, not Mr. Presley.

(All laugh, ABBY *and* BARBARA *a bit more.)*

CYNTHIA. Which is Colonel Tom's first question: "Whose idea is this?"

ABBY. Fair question. Mr. Allen's.

CYNTHIA. Second question: "Can Mr. Presley move around the pedestal?"

ABBY. No.

CYNTHIA. *(while writing)* No moving around pedestal.

ABBY. Because the dog's there. He's not going to gyrate around the dog. *(to* HOUND ONE*)* You don't want Elvis Presley gyrating around you, do you?

HOUND ONE. Woof.

CYNTHIA. Oh my.

HOUND TWO. Woof.

ABBY. I think they understand.

CYNTHIA. I think they disagree. Last question: "Can he ignore the dog…"

ABBY. He can't ignore the dog.

CYNTHIA. "…And sing to the audience?"

ABBY. He has to sing to the Hound Dog.

CYNTHIA. "Must sing to dog."

ABBY. He has to sing to the Hound Dog.

CYNTHIA. Okay.

ABBY. Cynthia, this was clearly stated in the memo.

CYNTHIA. Don't shoot, I'm the messenger.

ABBY. He's singing "You Ain't Nothing But A Hound Dog" to the Hound Dog. That's the deal.

CYNTHIA. Seems humorous on some level.

ABBY. Cynthia, this is the solution we've come up with so we don't have a replay of the June 5th, Milton Berle show. I'm sure you saw that.

CYNTHIA. I was there.

ABBY. Consensus is that he performed "You Ain't Nothing But a Hound Dog" with more bumps and grinds than a stripper.

CYNTHIA. It was…an event.

ABBY. NBC received so much mail and telephone on that, they're petrified. And correct me if I'm wrong, that was only his third TV appearance?

CYNTHIA. First on Jackie Gleason, second on Milton Berle.

ABBY. *(taking small envelope from pocket)* Oh…let's see how they respond to treats. I brought some. Would you like to give them some?

CYNTHIA. I'd love to. Thanks.

    *(**ABBY** give envelope to **CYNTHIA**.)*

ABBY. So it seems, Mr. Presley has become very comfortable on TV.

CYNTHIA. He's very relaxed.

    *(to **HOUND ONE**)*

    Here you go. Lay down.

ABBY. Well, I don't know if the word "relaxed" is the correct word.

CYNTHIA. *(to **HOUND ONE**)* Sit.

    *(to **ABBY**)* And you have the tuxedo?

ABBY. The tux is right here.

CYNTHIA. *(to **HOUND ONE**)* Beg.

ABBY. There will be Chandeliers in the background.

CYNTHIA. Oh, that's nice.

    *(to **HOUND ONE**)* Good girl.

    (gives treat)

ABBY. The dog picked will also have on a top hat, as will Mr. Presley.

CYNTHIA. *(writes)* Plus top hat.

ABBY. We're sure the audience will be tapping their feet, snapping their fingers, swaying with Mr. Presley.

CYNTHIA. The problem is that Mr. Presley does all of those things together.

(to **HOUND TWO***)*

Now your turn.

ABBY. Well, he's going to have to contain himself for this formal occasion where he is introduced to millions throughout the nation.

CYNTHIA. *(to* **HOUND TWO***)* Lay down.

ABBY. Cynthia, this is a tremendous opportunity, you must admit?

CYNTHIA. *(to* **HOUND TWO***)* Sit.

(to **ABBY***)* Well, everything that's been happening in the past year has been tremendous. In fact, Elvis' career has taken off so that no one can keep up with it. Especially since his first album just went Gold. Which is why I'm leaving. Actually, this is my last day.

ABBY. Oh, I'm sorry.

CYNTHIA. I'm not.

(to **HOUND TWO***)* Beg.

(to **ABBY***)* I have two children, I haven't seen in two months. I just want to go home. And I am tomorrow.

ABBY. That's understandable.

CYNTHIA. *(to* **HOUND TWO***)* Good girl.

(gives treat)

ABBY. Now Cynthia, we've heard Elvis may be going on the Ed Sullivan Show.

CYNTHIA. Tentative for September ninth.

ABBY. Well, congratulations on the tentative.

CYNTHIA. Thank you.

ABBY. And I've heard Ed Sullivan's not going to allow Mr. Presley to be filmed below the waist.

CYNTHIA. Well, that's why tonight's show is so important. If things go well here, The Sullivan show, which has a higher family draw, may allow filming of Presley completely.

ABBY. Our thoughts exactly.

CYNTHIA. And that's why you could probably ask Elvis to sing suspended from a rope, and the Colonel would go along with it.

ABBY. Well, I thank you and the Colonel for your honesty on this.

CYNTHIA. And that's also why, I think, they sent me. Cause they realize this is something they have to do, and they just want to do it and move on.

ABBY. Oh, and white gloves. He has to wear white gloves. They're in the tuxedo.

CYNTHIA. *(writes)* Plus white gloves.

(pause)

Okay. *(pause)* Presley will go out there with one of these Hound Dogs, sing to her, wear the tuxedo, but there is one thing that *we* request.

ABBY. And remember to tell the Colonel that we are agreeing to film Mr. Presley fully.

CYNTHIA. Yes. But there is one small thing Mr. Presley requests.

ABBY. Okay.

CYNTHIA. Mr. Presley would like to request that with his tuxedo…to be allowed to wear his…Blue Suede Shoes.

ABBY. *(long pause)* Perhaps we can work that in. *(thinks)* Consider it done.

CYNTHIA. Well, thank you. Let me take the tuxedo…leave the shoes.

ABBY. And do you care to cast a vote as to which dog to use?

CYNTHIA. No. They are both beautiful.

ABBY. Nice meeting you.

CYNTHIA. Nice meeting you.

BARBARA. Nice to meet you too, Cynthia.

CYNTHIA. Nice to meet you.

(CYNTHIA exits with tuxedo.)

BARBARA. Don't you have to run it by Mr. Allen about the blue suede shoes?

ABBY. Who cares?

BARBARA. It breaks formality.

ABBY. It's no big deal.

(**ABBY** *picks up phone, dials.*)

BARBARA. It may be just the opening that Presley needs to go nuts.

ABBY. It's a little thing.

(into phone)

Mr. Allen…Colonel Tom Parker's secretary was here. Not Elvis or Parker. And Elvis is going to be up there with the Hound dog, sing to it, wear the tuxedo, top hat, and all they had was one request. They requested that Elvis be allowed to wear his blue suede shoes. So I said okay.

(Smiles, long pause, smile drops.)

They are only Blue Suede Shoes! *(pause)* No, it's not an opening to go wild. *(pause)* No, he's not going. *(Stops suddenly. Pause.)* Steve?

(to **BARBARA***)*

He hung up.

(hangs up phone)

But not before he said Presley can wear 'em…as long as they're nailed to the floor.

(pause)

BARBARA. Okay. Then let's work on this other problem. What's this other guest's name?

ABBY. The other guest's name is: Jerry Lee Lewis. And the song he wants to sing is: "Great Balls Of Fire?"

BARBARA. "Great Balls of Fire?"

ABBY. Do you know what I think, Barbara? I think that Elvis Presley opened a very dangerous door on the Milton Berle show last month.

BARBARA. You can't *sing* "Great Balls Of Fire," on television. You can't *even say*, "Great balls of fire," on television.

ABBY. And I really don't think tuxedos or Hound Dogs are going to be able to close it.

HOUND DOG ONE. Woof.

HOUND DOG TWO. Woof.

ABBY. Yea, you tell them.

*(**ABBY** nods, "Yes," **BARBARA** shakes head, "No.")*

(Lights fade, End of Play.)

INTRO TO SCENE THREE: "3 A.M. IN THE GARDEN WITH A GOD"

(Lights fade in theatre, the following is heard.:)

RADIO VOICE. In sports, the AFL versus the NFL World Championship game at the Los Angeles Memorial Coliseum is only a few days away or as some are calling it: The Super Bowl. This is the first ever meeting between the two leagues and expectations of inequality are running high. The University of Arizona and the University of Michigan marching bands will be performing at halftime and even President Lyndon Johnson has an opinion on the game.

(trailing off) …Most news media and fans believe that the long established National Football league…

(Pause. Lights up on Scene Three.)

THREE A.M. IN THE GARDEN WITH A GOD

SET
Bare stage

TIME
January, 1967

PLACE
Memphis, Tennessee

CAST
Eve

3 A.M. IN THE GARDEN WITH A GOD was first produced by the Metropolitan Theatre Company in New York City as a selection of the Midtown International Theatre Festival, at the Where Eagles Dare Theatre, 347 West 36th Street on July 18th 2007. Executive producer, John Chatterton; managing director, Emileena Pedigo; artistic director, Glory Sims Bowen; marketing director, Bob Ost. The play was directed by Branan Whitehead; stage managed by Lloyd Fass; produced by Luigi Jannuzzi/ Branan Whitehead; lighting and sound design by Lloyd Fass and Branan Whitehead. The cast was as follows:

EVE . . . . ALISHA CAMPBELL

(Lights rise on **WOMAN**.*)*

WOMAN. I have this recurring dream that I am in the Garden of Paradise. *(pause)* And I am Eve. *(pause)* And Elvis Presley is Adam. *(pause)* And one day, he offered me an apple.

(pause)

AND I DOVE ON IT!

(pause, laughs)

But this dream is not in my imagination.

(pause)

Oh no.

(pause, nods)

It really did happen.

(pause)

Let me set the scene.

(pause)

It was around three a.m. A Sunday night. Raining. Windy. Terrible night. My hair under a hat, I'm wearing sweat pants, sneakers, sweat shirt that says "Sinatra." And I'm standing in line at this Memphis supermarket. I ran out to get milk, cereal, diapers… and I just got carried away. No one was there, my two kids sleeping, I couldn't sleep, I told my husband, "We need so much stuff, I'm going out." So I went wild,… up and down the aisles, even checking out stuff I neer look at cause, who cares, I have time. Finally, I'm at the checkout. I have a cart full. I mean, a gigantic cart full. And I remember, "Bananas, I forgot Bananas." And my kids have to have bananas. I, myself, have a potassium deficiency and try to eat one every day…so does my husband…we're basically big banana eaters. So I turn, and pushing my cart, head to the fruit aisle. And did you ever notice that the bananas are always way at the end of the fruit aisle? They put them there 'cause they want you to walk by all the fruit to get to the bananas. It's like the milk.

Ever notice they always put the milk at the furthest corner of any store so you have to walk past everything to get to the milk?

Well anyway, there they are, the bananas. And I reach, and I take a bunch, actually the last bunch, and I hear this voice say, "Miss, do you know...do you know, if there are anymore ba...ba..nanas?" I turn, there's a man there. A little frightening in this big empty store. And he's pointing to this now empty shelf of bananas, of which I am holding the last bunch of, about eight. A man with a black hat, black leather jacket, black pants, leather boots, and dark, can't see through, shades. And he's looking at my bananas. And I'm thinking, "I got here first, they're for my family, my potassium deficient family. And I really don't want to come back to the store tomorrow just for bananas. Which is what I'll have to do, if I give half to this man." Who, I notice, has no wedding ring on the hand with which he is pointing. So I figure, he's single. He can go out and get as many bananas as he wants, anytime he wants. Not like me who has, middle of the night, shopping sprees just to keep even with life as it's chasing me down. Or maybe...he's cheating a lot, and he forgot to put his wedding ring back on, having just come from his mistress' house, here at three a.m., wanting to have some bananas. Anyway, without making any judgments I say, "I don't know if there are anymore." And I casually start looking around, as if a banana bunch may be hiding in the mangos, or avocados. And I'm bobbing my head, clutching my banana bunch, lifting my neck, peering into, and over some pineapple, and I'm thinking, "Suppose he's a motorcycle freak, some wacko, and needs these for some initiation rite, and he's about to leave me stuck and bleeding in the fruit aisle, mumbling, "Help me, help me," as nectarines are bouncing off my head, and my life force is coursing out of me?" *(pause)*

So I quickly decide, that I am going to conclude with, "No, I don't see any," and then throw out a big... "BUT

SIR...why don't you take half of mine, is that fair, or do you need more?" 'Cause I am now thinking, "A contest over this bunch may get downright mean, I will not win, and I am not going down for a bunch of bananas and not very pleasant looking ones at that." And suddenly I notice this huge smile breaks on his face. And he says, "That's very kind of you, Miss, if I may have half." So I break the bunch. He says, "Thanks." I turn my cart around. And heading no more than a few steps, thinking, "I am out of here." "I am going where there is at least another person, like the checkout counter, where things are safe." Thinking, "Why do I even come out at three o'clock? And this is why there are no people out at three o'clock." Thinking, "How stupid am I?" *(pause)* When I hear behind me the words, "Excuse me though, Miss, may I ask you one more thing?" I stop. "May I ask you one more thing, Miss?" I freeze. My back still to the scary man. I scan the fruit dept in front of me, that is connected to the Deli department, that is connected to the Flower and Bakery department and there is no one, not a soul for aisles. And I turn and say, "Excuse me, Sir, what?" And he very politely says, "You seem to have the last jar of peanut butter, the kind I love...and I was wondering if." I look down. There it is...right on top. I grab the peanut butter, hold it out to him. "It's yours...take it, it's yours," I say. "I just took one, it doesn't matter to my 6 children," I say. And now I'm lying. I only have 2 children. But I figure, if he's thinking of killing me, right here,...right now, in front of the grapefruit, I want as much guilt as possible riding his dammed to hell soul into the eternal flames. "It doesn't matter to my 6 children," I say, "If they eat chunky or creamy." And he says, "Well, there are all types left, cause I was just over there, except...this kind.

So, if it doesn't matter? "It doesn't matter," I say, "It really doesn't matter. No, no, it doesn't matter." "I so appreciate it, I really do," he says. "Fine," I say, "Fine, and I am repeating: fine, fine." And he says, "Please don't be nervous, please don't...I don't mean to frighten you, Miss." And I'm saying, "Fine, I'm fine," as I'm clutching my cart now and I'm lying, 'cause I don't know what else to say cause I'm so nervous, and he's approaching me, he takes a step nearer to me and I'm on automatic response now, repeating over and over, just as unconvincing as I can, "Oh no, I'm really fine, very fine." So fine I could just cry, I'm fine." And then I start to cry. "I'm fine," I cry, "I'm fine, take the peanut butter, is there anything else you want, Mister, is there anything else you want?" And now I see this big lump forming in his throat. "Miss," he says, "Please, please calm down, I do not mean to frighten you. Here, why don't you take the bananas and the peanut butter." "I'm fine," I am crying, "I'm fine!"

And he says, "Please, please, Miss," as he backs away. And I cry louder, "Fine, I am fine." He puts the peanut butter and the bananas down, says, "Miss, please don't scream, please don't." "Fine, I'm fine, I'm fine," I'm saying. And he starts to say, "I'm sorry, I'm sorry." And now I'm saying, "I'm fine," and he's saying, "I'm sorry." And we are repeating, "I'm fine, I'm sorry, I'm fine, I'm sorry...I'm fine, fine, fine...I'm sorry, sorry, sorry." And he has his hands out. His hands are out, above his shoulders, as if he's just robbed a bank, been caught and someone has a gun in his back. He is profusely apologizing with his fingers spread wide open, I am clutching my cart. *(pause)* And then... it happens. *(pause)* He takes off his hat, he takes off his glasses, and he says, "Miss, my name is Elvis Presley, please do not scream or be frightened, and I wish you would accept my apology from the bottom of my heart." *(pause)* Now I'm looking at him. Now I realize it is Elvis Presley. And now, I let out the most blood curdling scream that has ever been heard in the state of Tennessee, let alone the Memphis Metropolitan area. AHHHHHHHHHHHHHHHHHH! *(pause)* Elvis rocks backwards on his heels. Elvis drops his hat. Elvis drops his glasses. An avalanche of apples, set off by the reverberation of this, comes caroming down on him, dominoing into the melons, that come rolling down. Elvis is knocked a little bit to the left and as he puts his hands out. Crouching a bit, he is pushed down by the mere weight of the fruit descending. Apples are now bounding off of his chest. He is on the ground and I am standing over top of him, screaming again, not because he frightened me, because I am no longer frightened at all, and not because he is Elvis, but rather because of what I have now done to this man, this king of Memphis, who has helped so many people, and children, who has given so much to so many, and here I have pelted him with apples and melons and notice that now the plums have begun a fresh assault upon his head. So I throw my body in front of the apples, trying to protect him. 'Cause he is down on the ground now, he is helpless. "Back," I say, "Back fruit, do you not know who this is?" I am trying to command them like God. "Stay away from him, apples," I shout, as if I am now Eve protecting the King from the forbidden fruit here in the garden at three am. And he is saying, "Miss, It's all right, I'm all right." And then I fall. And I'm falling backwards, falling and I feel these hands. These big hands. "I have you," I hear. At that point, I just let my body go. *(pause)* I let everything go. *(pause)* I could feel the plums, the apples, melons hitting my legs. And I fell...and I fell. And I looked up, and there was his face. Oh...I bet Eve never saw a face so sweet. His beautiful face, laughing, looking at me. And I'm thinking, "This is it. *(pause)* This is the highlight of my life." *(pause)* Three a.m., nobody sees it, nobody's going to believe it." And I looked up and he had an apple in his hand and he took a bite of it and handing it to me, said, "Would you like a taste?" *(pause)* And I did. *(pause)* Oh yes, I did! And the next thing I remember, we were at the checkout, which he insisted on paying for. He put the bags in my trunk. And then he said, "I'm very sorry once again." To which I replied, "I'm fine, I'm fine. To which he said, "Don't start that again, now!" And I didn't. Then he said, "Get in your car." And I did. And he said, "Start your car." And I did. And he said, "Now drive away." And I did. *(pause)* And the funny thing is...sometimes I ride by that store...but I have never gone back in that store. I can no longer go back in that store.

'Cause it is no longer a store...it is a holy shrine, a sacred grotto of fruits and vegetables. It is an oracle where once a God visited. Where inside, nothing will ever look the same...where inside, nothing could ever be the same...and where inside that garden...no apple will ever again...taste as sweet.

(Blackout. End of Play.)

INTRO TO SCENE FOUR: "WHEN NIXON MET ELVIS"

(Lights fade in theatre, the following is heard.)

RADIO VOICE. Army officials and President Nixon attempted today to refute critics in Congress who have charged that military intelligence operations aimed at citizens in the U.S. have become a threat to political liberty.

Both the Senate and the House of Representatives have passed legislation on a clean air bill that will require all automobiles to be 90 per cent free of pollution by 1976.

And the Supreme Court has ruled 5 to 4 in favor of lowering the voting age to 18 in Presidential...

(trailing off) ...and Congressional elections.

(Pause. Lights up on Scene Four.)

WHEN NIXON MET ELVIS

SET

Bare Stage, 3 chairs, 3 phone headsets

TIME

December 21, 1970

PLACE

The White House, Washington, DC

CAST

Alice

Beth

Cathy

WHEN NIXON MET ELVIS was first produced by the Metropolitan Theatre Company in New York City as a selection of the Midtown International Theatre Festival, at the Where Eagles Dare Theatre, 347 West 36th Street, on July 18th 2007. Executive producer, John Chatterton; managing director, Emileena Pedigo; artistic director, Glory Sims Bowen; marketing director, Bob Ost. The play was directed by Branan Whitehead; stage managed by Lloyd Fass; produced by Luigi Jannuzzi/ Branan Whitehead; lighting and sound design by Lloyd Fass and Branan Whitehead. The cast was as follows:

ALICE.....................................REBECCA BATEMAN.
BETH.....................................ALICHA CAMPBELL
CATHY...JESSICA ASCH*
Also appeared as **CATHY** ....JENNIFER BLEVINS

(Lights rise on **THREE SECRETARIES** *at three chairs:* **CATHY** *down right,* **ALICE** *down left,* **BETH** *center.)*

(Phone rings or buzzes on down left desk.)

ALICE. Morning, White House?

(pause)

It's December 21st, 1970. That's why you called the White House, to find out the date?

(pause)

Oh, I see. *(pause)* Well, let me tell you something about the northwest gate: document everything, who, the time, date, even a synopsis of your conversation. And good luck on your first day.

(pause)

Okay…aside from the date, what's the other problem?

(pause)

Elvis…Presley? *(pause)* Could you hold on for a moment?

(hits phone button)

(Lights rise on **BETH** *as center desk's phone rings.)*

BETH. Presidential Appointment Secretary, Dwight Chapin's office, can I help you?

ALICE. Beth?

BETH. What's up?

ALICE. Elvis….Presley's here. *(pause)* Did you hear me?

BETH. AHHHHH! Hold on.

*(*CATHY* hits phone button. Lights rise on* **CATHY** *as down right desk phone rings.)*

CATHY. President Richard Nixon's office, how may I help you?

BETH. Cathy?

CATHY. Beth, can I call you right back? I have to get an aspirin.

BETH. Elvis...Presley is here.

> (*pause*)

> Are you there?

CATHY. (*pause*) AHHHHH!

BETH. Hold on?

> (**CATHY** *hits button, back to* **ALICE**.)

> Alice, are you still there?

ALICE. Where'd you go?

BETH. I told Cathy. What's he want? Why's he here?

ALICE. I have no idea. I just thought I'd tell you since you have a bigger picture of him on your desk than your husband.

BETH. And right now, where is he?

ALICE. Northwest gate.

BETH. You left him standing at the northwest gate?

ALICE. I'll call you back.

> (**BETH** *back to* **CATHY**.)

BETH. She just left him standing at the northwest gate.

CATHY. What? Is she nuts?

BETH. I'll call you back.

> (**ALICE** *hits button*.)

ALICE. Northwest gate?

> (*pause*)

> Tell Mr. Presley that.

> (*pause*)

> What do you mean, "He's gone?"

> (*pause*)

> Where'd he go?

> (*pause*)

> You send that letter right in to me. I am right inside the main door, My name is Alice, I am head of operators. You tell that Marine to sprint! Do you hear me?

(Buzzer)

BETH. Alice?

ALICE. Beth, he's gone.

BETH. What?

ALICE. He left. I don't know.

BETH. I am holding you personally responsible.

ALICE. But he left a letter. The marine's bringing it in.

BETH. When you get it…call. I gotta call Cathy.

(Hits button. Cathy's phone rings. **ALICE** *rises, exits stage left.)*

CATHY. President Richard Nixon's Office.

BETH. Cath?

CATHY. I have no record. The Presidents' schedule's full. I'm looking at it.

BETH. I don't either, and Chapin would know, he's the appointment secretary, there's nothing on the calendar.

CATHY. It's exciting though.

BETH. But he's gone.

CATHY. Who?

BETH. Elvis.

CATHY. NOOOO.

BETH. He was there, now he's gone!

CATHY. Oh no, don't say that.

BETH. But he left a letter. It's on the way in.

CATHY. Beth?

BETH. Yea.

CATHY. Do you think this might not be Elvis?

BETH. I was thinking that.

CATHY. I mean, Elvis Presley, middle of winter, comes to Washington DC, walks to the northwest gate, leaves a letter?

BETH. It doesn't make sense, does it?

CATHY. No, it doesn't.

BETH. Oh well.

CATHY. Imagine if it was though?

BETH. Yea, imagine. Elvis just out of the blue.

(**ALICE** *runs in with letter. Hits phone buttons,* **BETH***'s phone rings.*)

BETH. Hold on.

ALICE. I got the letter!

BETH. Cath and I think it's an imposter. Here, let me put Cath on.

(pause)

Cath?

CATHY. Yea.

ALICE. Hi Cathy.

CATHY. Hi Alice.

BETH. I mean, Alice, it's the middle of winter.

ALICE. It was Elvis.

BETH. Alice?

ALICE. I have the letter.

BETH. Anyone can write a letter.

ALICE. The guard's certain, he's a big fan.

CATHY. Hey, I hope you're right, maybe it was Elvis.

ALICE. Thank you Cathy.

BETH. All right, let's say it was Elvis.

CATHY. Elvis had nothing to do.

BETH. So he came here from Memphis…in the middle of winter.

CATHY. With a velvet cape.

BETH. Just to drop off a letter at the gate. Yea, let's say he did that.

ALICE. I'm going to laugh at both of you when this turns out to be true.

CATHY. Read the letter.

ALICE. First of all it's written on American Airlines stationary.

BETH. Excuse me?

CATHY. Did you say, American Airlines stationary?

ALICE. In fact, on top there's a space to write the in flight: altitude and location.

CATHY. Alice, I think you should send that to security.

ALICE. Do you want me to read it, or not?

BETH. Go ahead.

CATHY. Then send it to security.

> (**BETH** *and* **CATHY** *laugh.*)

ALICE. "Dear Mr. President. First I would like to introduce myself. I am Elvis Presley.

BETH. That's enough proof for me.

CATHY. Yea, anything scribbled on official airline stationary.

ALICE. "I admire you and have great respect for you,… uh,…have great respect for your office." I'm sorry, it's scribbled, it's hard to read. "I talked to Vice President Agnew in Palm Springs three weeks ago."

BETH. Spiro *was* there, three weeks ago.

ALICE. See.

BETH. And he did meet Elvis, he told me.

ALICE. And how would this kook have known that?

BETH. It was in the paper.

CATHY. Wow, this is strange.

BETH. All weirdo's are strange. That's why they're called weirdo's.

ALICE. "I talked to Vice President Agnew and expressed my concern for our country."

BETH. What's he talking about?

ALICE. "The drug culture, the hippie elements, the S.D.S., Black Panthers, etc. do not," And "*NOT*" is underlined, "do *NOT* consider me as their enemy or as they call it The Establishment."

BETH. Elvis did not write this.

CATHY. He writes things like, "You ain't nothin' but a Hound dog," right?

ALICE. "Sir, I can and will be of any service that I can to help the country out. I have no concern or motives other than helping the country out."

BETH. He wants to battle hippies?

CATHY. I think of him almost like a hippy, I mean, he has long hair.

BETH. He is not a hippy.

CATHY. Does he have a crew cut?

ALICE. Will you two stop it? "So...I wish not to be given a title or an appointed position. I can and will do more good if I were made a Federal Agent at Large."

BETH. I'm lost. What does he want?

ALICE. He wants to be a Federal Agent.

CATHY. Elvis has appeared at the Northwest gate and wants to be a Federal Agent. That's what you want me to tell President Nixon?

(CATHY *laughs.*)

(BETH *laughs.*)

ALICE. "I am on this plane with Senator George Murphy and we have been discussing the problems that our country is faced with. Sir, I am staying at the Washington Hotel, Room 505, 506, 507."

CATHY. What's he need three rooms for?

BETH. Maybe he brought a lot of guitars.

CATHY. I think it's for whoever this is and his multiple personalities.

ALICE. "I have two men who work with me by the name of Jerry Schilling and Sonny West. I am registered under the name of Jon Burrows."

CATHY. You know what I think. I don't think it's Elvis, it's Jon Burrows. And I think this guy Jon Burrows thinks he's Elvis. That's what I think.

ALICE. "I will be here for as long as long as it takes to get the credentials of a Federal Agent. I have done an in-depth study of drug abuse."

CATHY. What is this guy babbling about?

ALICE. "And Communist brainwashing techniques and I am right in the middle of the whole thing."

CATHY. What whole thing?

ALICE. "Where I can and will do the most good."

CATHY. Elvis has done a study of Communist Brainwashing techniques? Give it to security, Alice.

BETH. This is really wacko, Alice.

ALICE. Okay, Beth...I'm going to send this up to you.

(Light fade. Phone rings. Pause.)

(Lights up to signify time passing. **BETH** *waiting,* **ALICE** *answers.)*

ALICE. White House.

BETH. Alice.

ALICE. What'd you find out?

BETH. Hold on. Let me get Cath.

*(***CATHY***'s phone rings.)*

CATHY. President Nixon's.

BETH. Cathy.

CATHY. Who's here now? Neil Diamond?

BETH. Listen...Graceland says he's at the Washington Hotel 505 to 507, Washington Hotel says it's Presley, Senator George Murphy talked to him on the plane. It checked out, it all checked out. Dwight and Bud were going to push Presley off on the Vice President and I said, "Over my dead body." They agreed and Bud is meeting with Presley right here, right now. I can see him.

CATHY. AHHHH,

ALICE. It is Elvis?

BETH. It's all true.

CATHY. The letter?

BETH. All of it.

ALICE. Is this a riot!

BETH. Bud is in there talking to him about drugs and what Presley can do. And he had me calling all over trying to find some kind of honorary agent-at-large credential. That's why I couldn't call either one of you, I had to go over to the FBI building where they print these up. Nixon's gonna sign it. It's unbelievable.

ALICE. So what's Presley wearing?

CATHY. Yea, what's he wearing?

BETH. I'm looking right at him.

ALICE. Did you meet him?

BETH. I met him. Shook his hand.

CATHY. My gosh.

ALICE. I can't believe it.

BETH. Okay, he has these really tight velvet pants on.

CATHY. No.

BETH. Yea.

ALICE. Wow.

CATHY. He's not wearing a normal business suit?

BETH. No! He has this silky flowing shirt on.

ALICE. What color?

BETH. White.

ALICE. How about the collar?

BETH. A big high collar.

CATHY. You're kidding me.

BETH. It's open down to his chest.

ALICE & BETH. NOOO!

BETH. Yea, with this big gold medallion. I think he shampoos his chest hairs just so the medallion will bounce.

ALICE & BETH. *(Laugh.)*

BETH. Oh God is he sexy?

ALICE. Is he?

BETH. And remember you mentioned about the cape?

CATHY. Yea.

BETH. He's got the cape.

ALICE. No.

BETH. A big dark purple cape. It's unbelievable.

CATHY. Is it velvet?

BETH. It's velvet. It matches his pants.

ALICE & CATHY. NOOOO!

BETH. And sunglasses on. With an EP over the nose bridge. And around his waist.

ALICE. Yea.

CATHY. Yea.

BETH. He's got this huge belt buckle, it must be 5 by 7 inches, with this gold design. Dwight was like…what is that? And it has something written on it.

CATHY. What's it say?

BETH. I don't know, I'm not going to stick my face in Presley's crotch to read it.

ALICE. I would.

BETH. Stop it.

CATHY. How bout the sideburns?

BETH. Huge.

ALICE. And the hair?

BETH. Beautiful. Long, black. And you know what, he really should get it cut.

CATHY. Does he look like a hippy a bit?

BETH. Well, it's below his ears but he is not a hippy.

CATHY. So is he coming over here. What's up?

BETH. Yea! Yea!

CATHY. What time?

BETH. We put him…12:15.

CATHY. 12:15. Elvis is coming here. I can't believe it, I'm going to get to meet Elvis Presley.

ALICE. I can't believe it.

CATHY. I need a camera.

BETH. Oh, by the way, Dwight has me typing up a memo to the guard, you, Alice, it's confidential, not a word.

CATHY. Oh no.

BETH. Yup. Mum, the whole thing, cause he's going to be a Federal Agent at Large. Suppose that got out?

ALICE. Oh my God, Nixon is going to meet Elvis. This is so unreal and we can't tell anybody?

BETH. No, and they have this idea that Presley's going to turn this whole drug war around.

ALICE. You're kidding me?

BETH. Listen to these two wacky ideas that Bud's come up with. "One: He wants to create this "Hour television special in which Presley narrates as stars such as himself sing popular songs and interpret them for parents in order to show drug and other anti-establishment themes in rock music."

ALICE. Are you reading this?

BETH. Yea. And two: He's going to get Presley to "encourage fellow artists to develop a new rock musical with the theme, "Get High on Life."

(They all laugh.)

CATHY. That's ridiculous.

ALICE. That's the stupidest thing I've ever heard.

BETH. And here's the kicker. They want Presley to "Record an album."

ALICE. What?

BETH. And they want a "Get high on life theme."

ALICE. Oh God.

BETH. And they want it recorded at the Federal narcotics rehabilitation Facility in Lexington, Kentucky.

ALICE & CATHY. Eweeee.

BETH. Can you believe it?

CATHY. Who wants to hear that?

ALICE. I want to hear love songs.

BETH. I know. Who wants to hear Elvis sing about heroin?

(They all laugh.)

CATHY. What an idiot.

BETH. Is that funny or what?

    (Lights fade. Phone rings. Pause.)

    (Lights up to signify time passing. **CATHY** *waiting.* **BETH** *answers.)*

BETH. Appointment Secretary Dwight Chapin's office.

CATHY. Beth?

BETH. Is he there?

CATHY. Yes. Hold on.

    *(***CATHY*** *dials.* ***ALICE****'s phone rings.* ***ALICE*** *answers.)*

ALICE. White House.

BETH. Alice?

ALICE. He's there?

CATHY. He's here. He's here. I shook his hand. It was great. It was all I could do not to take a picture. Anyway, I can see them right now. He's in there with Dick. He's standing there with Dick.

ALICE. Wow!

CATHY. They're taking pictures. This is so weird. I am looking at this. This is history, I think.

ALICE. Really?

CATHY. Yea, I mean, Elvis is shaking hands with Dick.

BETH. You're kidding me.

CATHY. No, they're standing in front of these four flags. I'm looking right in. It's unbelieveable. Look at Dick and Elvis.

ALICE. Wow.

BETH. Wow.

CATHY. Unbelievable. Oh, he is cute. He is so cute.

ALICE. What are they doing?

CATHY. Well, Presley's showing Dick a bunch of police badges he brought with him. Let me listen.

ALICE. Badges?

CATHY. Colorado, Tennessee. He's got honorary badges. And Dick is really enthused.

BETH. I didn't think he was a fan.

CATHY. Oh, oh. Dick's pointing at Presley. And Presley's looking down.

BETH. What's he saying?

CATHY. Oh, oh, Presley said something about the Beatles.

BETH. I hate the Beatles.

CATHY. I like them.

ALICE. What do you have against the Beatles?

CATHY. Something about the Beatles being out for money...then they returned to England and they're anti-American.

BETH. Who said that?

CATHY. Elvis.

ALICE. Huh...Elvis is against the Beatles, I didn't know that.

CATHY. Now Presley's telling him..."I'm on your side." He's getting kind of emotional too.

BETH. Who Nixon?

CATHY. No, Presley. Nixon doesn't have emotions. Yea, yea...he's saying, "I'm on your side, I'm on your side." And Dick is nodding. And Presley's saying: "He's poor, he's a poor boy."

(pause) Whoa, hey.

ALICE. What?

BETH. What?

CATHY. He's got a gun.

ALICE. Who?

CATHY. Elvis' got a gun.

BETH. What are you talking about?

CATHY. It looks like a pistol. He's giving it to Nixon. Nixon is...Whoa! Nixon's nodding. He likes it.

BETH. Really?

ALICE. I can't believe he brought a gun in there.

CATHY. Yea, why'd he give him a gun?

BETH. I bet that gun ends up in his Yorba Linda library.

ALICE. Yea, I bet ya.

CATHY. Oh no.

ALICE. What?

CATHY. Bud closed the door.

ALICE. Why?

CATHY. I don't know. Don't close the door, I can't hear.

BETH. Oh.

ALICE. Noooo.

CATHY. They closed the door.

ALICE & BETH. No.

CATHY. But I have one last revelation for you. And I just got it delivered to my desk just before I called.

BETH. What?

ALICE. What?

CATHY. In ten minutes, Bud is taking Elvis to lunch in the White House dining room. AND WE ARE GOING!

BETH. YES!

ALICE. What about me?

BETH. What about Alice? How can we get Alice in?

CATHY. Alice, I got a press pass from Bud coming right down to you.

ALICE. You're kidding me.

CATHY. Nope. And I got Bud to introduce us.

BETH. YEA!

ALICE. YES!

BETH. Oh…oh Cathy I owe you.

CATHY. I know.

ALICE. Thank you, Cathy.

BETH. Thank you Cath.

ALICE. Thank you so much.

CATHY. You're both welcome. Alice, start heading up right now, I'll send the pass down with one of the Marines, I'll meet you over at the dining room.

ALICE. This is the greatest day of my life.

BETH. I think this is the greatest day in Nixon's career too.

CATHY. Oh stop it.

ALICE. I think so too.

CATHY. This has little to do with being a President, serving the country.

BETH. It's historical. It's strange, weird and...historical.

CATHY. What about this trip to China he's planning?

BETH. Nope.

CATHY. What bombing Cambodia? That was historic.

BETH. No, I think the history books are going to write this day was it, when Nixon met Elvis.

CATHY. That is the stupidest thing I've ever heard.

BETH. I wouldn't doubt that Nixon sells that picture, at his gift shop at Yorbo Lindal, a it's one of the biggest souvenirs that anyone buys.

ALICE. Cathy, this is Elvis. People are going to forget Nixon, but they're going to listening to Elvis for years. Think about it.

CATHY. He's a singer. Nixon meets with leaders of countries. You think this photograph is going to top hundreds of rulers on this Earth with whom Nixon has dealt?

ALICE & BETH. YEA!

(All laugh.)

CATHY. Okay, ten minutes.

ALICE. Ten minutes.

BETH. Ten minutes.

CATHY. *(pause)* 'Till Elvis.

(ALICE's phone rings.)

ALICE. Hold on.

(ALICE hits button.)

White House, can I help you?

(BETH's phone rings.)

BETH. Hold on.

(**BETH** *hits button.*)

Presidential Appointment Secretary, Dwight Chapin's office, how can I help you?

(**CATHY**'*s phone rings.*)

CATHY. Hold on.

(**CATHY** *hits phone button.*)

President Richard Milhous Nixon's office, how may I help you?

(*Blackout. End of play.*)

INTERMISSION

ACT II

*INTRO TO SCENE FIVE: "WARHOL EXPLAINS ART TO
ELVIS"*

(Lights fade in theatre, the following is heard:)

RADIO VOICE. In sports today, Jack Nicklaus has become the youngest player ever to win the Masters Golf Championship at Augusta, Georgia at the age of 23.

In entertainment, the motion picture Academy Award winner for Best Film this year is *Lawrence of Arabia.*

And the first Pop Art Exhibit is in full swing in New York City. Many critics have proclaimed this is not Art, but Pop Artists, like Andy Warhol, seem to have gathered a following that enjoy this new off beat highly criticized exhibit.

(trailing off) …In other news…

(Pause. Lights up on Scene Five.)

WARHOL EXPLAINS ART
TO ELVIS

SET
Bare Stage, 2 chairs

TIME
April, 1963

PLACE
New York City

CAST
Allie
Bonny
Cindy

WARHOL EXPLAINS ART TO ELVIS was first produced by the Metropolitan Theatre Company in New York City as a selection of the Midtown International Theatre Festival, at the Where Eagles Dare Theatre, 347 West 36th Street, on July 18, 2007. Executive producer, John Chatterton; managing director, Emileena Pedigo; artistic director, Glory Sims Bowen; marketing director, Bob Ost. The play was directed by Branan Whitehead; stage managed by Lloyd Fass; produced by Luigi Jannuzzi/Branan Whitehead; lighting and sound design by Lloyd Fass and Branan Whitehead. The cast was as follows:

ALLIE . . . . JESSICA ASCH*

BONNY . . . . REBECCA BATEMAN

CINDY . . . . ALISHA CAMPBELL

*Also appeared as **ALLIE** . . . . JENNIFER BELVINS

(Lights rise on three young woman:)

(**CINDY** *is sitting in chair with back to audience.* **BONNY** *is pacing in front of chair that* **CINDY** *is sitting in.* **ALLIE** *is standing to side with clipboard and pencil.)*

ALLIE. Ready? *(pause)* Go.

BONNY. *(to* **CINDY***)* Simply.

ALLIE. Good start.

BONNY. Quite simply, Elvis.

ALLIE. *(takes buzzer sound)* Mr. Presley.

BONNY. Quite simply, Mr. Presley.

CINDY. *(sounding like Elvis)* Uh Huh.

BONNY. The reason why Andy.

ALLIE. *(buzzer sound)* Mr. Warhol.

BONNY. I meant "The reason why Mr. Warhol."

ALLIE. Okay.

BONNY. Would like you to sell.

ALLIE. *(buzzer sound)* We're selling, Presley's endorsing.

BONNY. The reason why Mr. Warhol would like you to endorse his portrait of you.

CINDY. *(sounding like Elvis)* Uh Huh.

ALLIE. Perfect.

BONNY. Is because you personify the phallic implications of secular iconography.

CINDY. *(sounding like Elvis)* WHAT?

ALLIE. *(makes buzzer sound)*

BONNY. It's true.

CINDY. *(stands)* My turn.

BONNY. Is it not true?

ALLIE. *(to* **CINDY***.)* Use what Bonny said, up to "because."

CINDY. Okay.

BONNY. You're trying to tell me that Andy didn't pick Elvis holding that gun because it's phallic?

ALLIE. I don't think phallic is the issue.

BONNY. Yes it is.

CINDY. And neither is iconography.

BONNY. This is an Icon, as sure as Andy was raised in a Pittsburgh Byzantine Church.

ALLIE. Not for what we're doing.

BONNY. All right, do what you want, forget art.

ALLIE. I'm afraid Presley's not going to know what Andy is talking about.

BONNY. That's the point. Intimidate him.

CINDY. That is Andy's charm.

ALLIE. Intimidation as a sales technique?

BONNY. And Presley's Baptist, he won't have a clue what iconography is.

   (**BONNY** *and* **CINDY** *laugh.*)

ALLIE. Let's start from, "Because."

BONNY. (**BONNY** *sits in Elvis chair*) Okay.

CINDY. I'm ready.

ALLIE. (*pause*) Set...go.

CINDY. Simply, Mr. Presley...Mr. Warhol would like you to endorse his portrait of you because he has already done.

ALLIE. Completed.

CINDY. He has already completed: Troy Donahue, Liz Taylor.

ALLIE. Elizabeth Taylor.

CINDY. Doesn't saying "Liz" show we're on a first name basis?

ALLIE. Elizabeth shows respect, more important than a first name basis.

CINDY. Elizabeth Taylor, Marilyn Monroe...and he would like to add you to his collection.

ALLIE. (*does Buzzer sound*) Elvis does not need to be added to anyone's collection.

CINDY. Andy.

ALLIE. Mr. Warhol.

CINDY. Mr. Warhol would like to immortalize you.

ALLIE. *(buzzer)*

CINDY. The reason why Mr. Warhol would like you to endorse his portrait of you is because you'll both make a lot of money.

ALLIE. *(buzzer)* Elvis doesn't need money, Andy's making it off of him.

BONNIE. Okay, okay, I got it.

    (**BONNIE** *stands to switch with* **CINDY**.)

CINDY. I got one sentence in, didn't I?

ALLIE. You did fine. Be Elvis.

    (**BONNY** *and* **CINDY** *switch.*)

BONNIE. Simply, Mr. Presley...Mr. Warhol would like you to endorse his portrait of you. He has already completed: Troy Donahue, Elizabeth Taylor, Marilyn Monroe. Period.

ALLIE. Perfect.

CINDY. I thought we need a reason.

BONNIE. They are silkscreen batches. And they are all silver.

ALLIE. I don't think he's going to know what a silkscreen is.

BONNIE. He may, and if he doesn't, it just gives him a little more information. But more importantly it serves as a smoke screen covering up the reason, "why?"

CINDY. OH.

ALLIE. I see.

CINDY. Good idea.

ALLIE. *(to* **BONNIE***)* Oh, by the way, Andy told me that you ruined a lot of the Elvis stuff.

BONNIE. I did not ruin any of the Elvis stuff. Andy thought I was making mistakes, not being perfect, so as to make them look artistic.

ALLIE. He said he thought you were making smudges to be impressionistic.

BONNIE. I couldn't handle the squeegee. You know how heavy they are.

ALLIE. Well,...why I bring it up is because, don't worry about it, all the Elvis silkscreens were destroyed.

BONNIE. What?

ALLIE. When it poured last week, that old firehouse he rented had a hole in the roof.

BONNIE. No.

ALLIE. Yea.

BONNIE. Why didn't Andy tell me?

ALLIE. Andy did them all over his own way.

BONNIE. This is what bothers me. We're trying to convince Elvis that Andy's going to immortalize him, when it isn't even art.

CINDY. Oh course it's art.

BONNIE. It's not only cookie cutter mentality, but if there *are* any differences between them, he throws them out.

ALLIE. Well, that's his art.

CINDY. It's Andy art.

BONNIE. Yea, it's Andy Art. And it's going to catch up with him.

CINDY. *(to ALLIE)* Did you tell her what Andy did to the Elvis images?

ALLIE. No.

BONNIE. What?

CINDY. *(to ALLIE)* You didn't tell her about the cutting?

ALLIE. No.

BONNIE. What about the cutting?

CINDY. He send the roll of Presley images and a bunch of stretcher bars to the Ferus gallery, and told the owner Irving Blum to cut them...any way he wanted.

BONNIE. No.

ALLIE. Yea. Andy said, "Just make sure they cover all the walls." Can you imagine any other artist doing that?

CINDY. Though I like this image that Andy's created. It shows Elvis with that gun, holster, hunting knife... and with Andy's image over image it looks like Elvis is moving.

BONNIE. Oh, Cindy…you don't know?

CINDY. Know what?

ALLIE. About the image.

CINDY. What about the image?

BONNIE. *(pause)* You tell her.

ALLIE. You don't know that Andy didn't paint the image?

CINDY. He didn't?

BONNIE. No.

CINDY. He didn't paint Elvis?

ALLIE. No.

CINDY. Well, where did he get it from?

BONNIE. A photograph.

CINDY. He did not!

ALLIE. He did.

BONNIE. It's a photograph from a publicity still.

CINDY. You are telling me…that Andy pirated it?

BONNIE. From a 60's western, called…what was the name of it?

ALLIE. *Flaming Star.*

BONNIE. *Flaming Star.*

CINDY. That is unbelievable.

BONNIE. Andy just blew it up, superimposed it on a silk-screen.

CINDY. *(gasps)*

ALLIE. I know.

CINDY. It's at a point where he's not even creating the initial image?

BONNY. And he's not even cutting them.

ALLIE. Irving said, "It didn't look like Art."

BONNIE. Well it's essentially a photograph on a silkscreen, cut by a gallery owner.

ALLIE & BONNIE & CINDY. *(laugh)*

CINDY. Oh, we are hitting low.

ALLIE. We go lower. Tell her about Bob Dylan.

BONNIE. You tell her.

ALLIE. It's your story.

BONNIE. Well…Andy gave one of the Silver Elvis' to Bob Dylan. And you know what Dylan did?

ALLIE. Traded it to his agent Albert Grossman.

CINDY. No.

BONNIE. For a sofa.

ALLIE & BONNIE & CINDY. *(laugh)*

ALLIE. All right, enough about the lack of quality, let's try to sell Elvis.

CINDY. Okay, I'm up, I'm up.

ALLIE. Uh…okay, take it from the top, last version. Ready?

CINDY. Ready.

ALLIE. Go.

CINDY. Quite simply, Mr. Presley…Mr. Warhol would like you to endorse his portrait of you. He has already completed: Troy Donahue, Elizabeth Taylor, Marilyn Monroe. They are silkscreen batches. And they are all silver.

ALLIE. All right, we need one more sentence to close.

CINDY. How about: It will be hanging in a gallery.

ALLIE. Prestigious.

BONNY. How about: Pretentious?

CINDY. It will be hanging in a prestigious gallery in New York City. It will garner international attention.

ALLIE. Oh, that's good.

CINDY. By Art magazines and appreciative fans.

ALLIE. Very good.

BONNIE. *(stands)* Raising you up to the phallic image that you are.

ALLIE. *(buzzer sound)*

    (BONNIE sits.)

CINDY. Raising your "star" to the "superstar" that you are.

BONNIE. Good.

CINDY. Where even Bob Dylan has admired the value.

ALLIE. Great.

CINDY. Of these silver Elvis.

ALLIE. Portraits.

CINDY. These silver Elvis portraits.

ALLIE. Okay, that's a wrap. One more letter to send out on the Elvis and Liz show. Elizabeth Taylor.

BONNIE. I'm Liz.

CINDY. All right.

ALLIE. Who wants to be Andy? You, me?

CINDY. I'll be Andy.

ALLIE. You're Andy. Now remember, with Liz it's stage, sophisticated,...Art. Very involved.

CINDY. I'm ready.

ALLIE. Ready?

BONNIE. Ready.

ALLIE. Ready. *(pause)* Go.

(Sudden Blackout. End of Play.)

INTRO TO SCENE SIX: "PINK CADILLACS AND GOD"

(Lights fade in theatre, the following is heard:)

RADIO VOICE. In the news…Democratic Candidate Jimmy Carter has defeated incumbent President Gerald Ford in an election that split the nation in half from the east to the west. Carter won 23 states and Washington DC. Ford took 27 states but not the large electorial states. And so Jimmy Carter becomes the first man from the deep south to be elected president since the civil war. *(trailing off)* …Jimmy Carter…

(Pause. Lights up on Scene Six.)

PINK CADILLACS AND GOD

SET
Bare Stage

TIME
November, 1976

PLACE
In or near Memphis, Tennessee

CAST

LORA

MONA

PAULA or **PAUL** *(if male)*

PINK CADILLACS AND GOD was first produced by the Metropolitan Theatre Company in New York City as a selection of the Midtown International Theatre Festival, at the Where Eagles Dare Theatre, 347 West 36th Street, on July 18, 2007. Executive producer, John Chatterton; managing director, Emileena Pedigo; artistic director, Glory Sims Bowen; marketing director, Bob Ost. The play was directed by Branan Whitehead; stage managed by Lloyd Fass; produced by Luigi Jannuzzi/Branan Whitehead; lighting and sound design by Lloyd Fass and Branan Whitehead. The cast was as follows:

LORA . . . . ALISHA CAMPBELL

MONA . . . . REBECCA BATEMAN

PAULA *(Female) or* **PAUL** *(Male)* . . . . CRAIG CLARY

(Lights rise on **LORA** *and* **MONA** *quietly screaming at each other.)*

LORA. I saw him first.

MONA. You did not.

LORA. I saw him when he drove on the lot.

MONA. Well, I was the first one out the door. How was I to know you saw him?

LORA. Cause I'm telling you.

MONA. He is my customer.

LORA. He is my customer.

*(***PAULA*** enters.)*

PAULA. All right, Ladies! Ladies, calm down! First of all, we have a customer in our showroom, who does not appreciate this. And as your manager, I will not tolerate this.

LORA. Sorry.

MONA. Sorry.

LORA. She's wrong.

MONA. She's wrong.

PAULA. How many cars has he bought off of you?

LORA. 52.

PAULA. And how many cars has be bought off of you?

MONA. 47.

PAULA. Who did he buy the last car off?

MONA. I don't think that's important.

LORA. Her.

PAULA. Did either one of get a phone call that he was coming in to see you?

LORA. No.

MONA. No.

PAULA. Either one of you sending him mailings on specials?

MONA. Every week.

LORA. I've been sending every week, too.

MONA. But it was my turn, I had the next customer.

LORA. You just had that old guy that looked at that bomb out there.

MONA. He had a question about tires, not sales. That doesn't count.

PAULA. Hold on! What I'm concerned with, is that we have a customer out there, who has purchased almost one hundred cars, wasting his time, while you are wasting your time arguing about who's going to do something, that we're not going to be able to do cause we're running out of time. Now I'm going to propose a solution.

LORA. I can make the sale, I know what he wants. He wants that pink Cadillac. And I need the commission.

MONA. Well, I know he wants the green truck, too. I can sell him that pink Cadillac and the green truck. And I need the commission just as bad. Don't let her tell you she has more children. She has a husband, I don't.

PAULA. I'm going to propose a solution, and the solution is…whoever answers this question best will go first.

LORA. Fair enough.

MONA. Okay.

PAULA. Fine. And the question is: "How can you, by making this sale, best help this company?" That's the question and I want an answer now.

MONA. May I go first? I'm ready.

LORA. Go right ahead.

PAULA. Go on.

MONA. Well, I will best be able to help this company because I am going to have a photographer take a picture, perhaps of all of us, and put it in the paper showing that we have now sold him 100 cars.

LORA. *(gasps)* I can't believe you did that.

MONA. What?

LORA. I can't believe she did that. That was my idea.

MONA. Was not.

LORA. Two days ago I said when we get the next sale we should say we sold him 100 cars.

MONA. All you said was that it was going to be our one hundredth car. You just added it up. It was my idea to put it in the newspaper.

LORA. No, you said, "Put it on television." I said, "Put it in the newspaper."

MONA. It's the same thing.

LORA. It is not.

PAULA. All right, stop. You've both come up with a good idea. It's basically both of yours. Okay, so that's not going to work.

LORA. Oh no, he's going near the door.

(They all look.)

MONA. Mr. Presley, don't go out that door.

LORA. We're going to lose this sale, I know we're going to lose this sale.

PAULA. He's just going to the water cooler, I can see him. Now, I want you to turn around. Turn around, both of you.

(They turn.)

Cause I have one more idea on how to decide this.

LORA. Okay.

MONA. What is it?

PAULA. All right, this is how we're going to decide who is going to sell Mr. Presley that pink Cadillac.

MONA. I can sell him the green truck too.

PAULA. Obviously, you've both sold him so many cars, you both know what he likes and the reasons. Well, I want you to tell me your theory why he buys…and the best explanation is going to get a chance to sell him another.

MONA. May I go first again? It's a cake question for me.

LORA. Go right ahead.

PAULA. Go on, Mona.

MONA. It's because he's such a good looking, conservative man.

LORA. He's a gorgeous man.

PAULA. One at a time, Mona's first.

MONA. Dresses well, got enough money to choke a horse, got a nice wife. And that's why so many women throw themselves at him. But because he's so conservative, I think this is his way, his civilized way of,...how should I put it. See, I think he regards the cars as women,...and that's why he loves to buy soft color ones, like power blue and pink.

LORA. Do you know I thought that too.

MONA. You're not going to say the same thing again, are you?

LORA. No.

MONA. Then will you let me finish?

LORA. Go ahead.

MONA. And that's why he looks at these cars so sexually.

PAULA. He does?

MONA. He does.

LORA. It's true he does talk kind of sexual.

MONA. For instance, he always refers to the car as "she." "She's beautiful, she's gorgeous."

LORA. That's exactly how he talks.

MONA. It's even funny cause at the end he always says, "Yea, I like her, I'd like to have her."

PAULA. And you don't think you're reading a little into this?

MONA. Oh no. Not the way he says it, it has another meaning.

LORA. It does.

MONA. I know it does. And that other meaning is not exactly...automotive. In fact, most time, it's enough to drive me wild! So anyway, that's the approach I take. And I even find myself saying things like, "She is one beautiful Lady," and "Any man would love to have her." And that's why I think he's bought over 600 cars around this area. 'Cause he just loves to walk in and say, "I want that one. I want to drive that one now!" I think it's very sexual. In fact, it's so sexual, sometimes, I wish I wasn't the salesperson…but the car. Well, anyway, that's my reason.

PAULA. *(to* **MONA***)* Very good.

(to **LORA***)*

You're going to have to top that. I don't know how you're going to top that.

LORA. I'm going to top that.

PAULA. Okay.

LORA. What's he doing out there now?

MONA. What's he doing?

PAULA. Sitting in the pink Cadillac. Oh, look at him sitting in the back seat.

MONA. Can I go sit in the back seat with him?

LORA. Paula, I'm ready for my answer.

PAULA. Sure, go ahead.

LORA. Well, I use to think it was about women. Cause he'd come in, rubbing, touching everything saying, "I love the leather, I love how she purrs." But I don't think that's what it is, and I've sold more cars to him.

MONA. Five more.

LORA. Whatever. But I don't know if you've ever noticed, but see what he's doing right now…staring at the hood? He always stares at the hood and grits his teeth. Then he stands in the front, just like he's doing right now cause, I think, he wants to see what the impact is. How this car's going to look coming at you. Then he shifts to the side.

PAULA. Oh my God, he did.

LORA. See…he shifts to the side. And he walks a little bit.

PAULA. He is.

LORA. As if it's passing you.

PAULA. Wow.

LORA. 'Cause I think it's about being religious.

MONA. Religious?

LORA. Yea, I think it's about being a man of God and the impact of inspiration. 'Cause notice there are two things he loves: Headlights and Convertibles. And that's cause...number one, he wants light to show "I'm the light coming at ya." You gotta remember here is a man raised in Gospel music. So when he's driving this car, he wants to see what the impact of his inspiration is on you. And that's why he checks the headlights. He wants large, bright headlights. And two: he wants a convertible. Cause he wants to see the sky, look up and say, "God, you, gave me this talent, and I'm using it." As if God could reach down, kiss him on his head, and say, "Good job, Elvis." And as for the color pink, it's alive! The black looks great, the white looks wonderful. But a pink, Caddy, convertible with huge bright lights,...Oh Man! And I even find myself saying things, to him, like, "Inspiring, isn't it?" Or "Perfection, that's what this is on four wheels." And that's why I don't think it's about women. I think it's about being a man of God and the impact of inspiration.

PAULA. Whoa! That was great. I don't know what to pick, those are two great answers. I love the woman. And I love the religious.

LORA. Paula, you have to make a decision.

MONA. Quick.

(They all turn and look.)

LORA. Where'd he go?

MONA. He's gone!

PAULA. He's looking at the tire.

LORA. OH! Thank God.

PAULA. I see his feet.

LORA. Hallelujah.

PAULA. Okay, okay...turn around, turn around! This is going to do it. I just thought of this and this is going to do it. There's no way there could be a tie on this.

MONA. Okay.

LORA. What is it?

PAULA. I am going to divide your commission in half.

LORA. What?

PAULA. And each one is going to get half a sale.

MONA. Why?

PAULA. So you are going to have 47 and a half sales, and you are going to have 52 and a half sales.

LORA. That's not fair.

MONA. That's not.

PAULA. Listen to me. It's going to be fair. This is my Solomon theory of sales. I'm going to divide it in half, but I want each one of you to decide who is the best to sell him that car. Cause your half is going to be dependant on the other's sales technique. So knowing what she's like today. And knowing what she's like today. Knowing what he wants to buy and knowing how you can sell…how you feel and what's going in the air…who would you pick to sell it, you or her…you or her?

LORA. How did you think of this?

PAULA. I don't know.

MONA. Personally, if we're going to do that, I would rather have her sell it.

LORA. I'm shocked.

PAULA. You would?

MONA. Especially if she can sell the truck too, cause today her attitude is more like a truck.

LORA. I'll take that as a compliment.

MONA. It's meant as a compliment. I drive one, love em'. They're tough, persistent.

LORA. All right, on the other hand, I think I'd like her to sell it. Cause she's just a little more aggressive today. She has more "want," cause she needs more money today.

PAULA. All right.

LORA. And I have another reason I'd rather have her sell it. She's looking very good today. She's dressed up, just had her nails and hair done and I haven't. She may have a better chance.

PAULA. Okay. So if you're going to share, each of you want the other one to do the work? All right then. Then I've made my decision.

MONA. You have?

LORA. How could you?

PAULA. First, I love how you think about this company and the idea you both came up with for the newspapers. Great idea, we're going to do that.

(pause)

Second, I love your theories on why he loves cars. No wonder you're such great saleswomen.

(pause)

Third, I love your answers on the commission. That's very nice to think that the other person has more strength, or looks prettier today. It's wonderful that you know so much about each other, and the confidence you have in each other.

(pause)

And it's because of that, and of all three wonderful responses, that I have decided that...neither one of you are going to make the sale.

LORA. Why not?

MONA. That's not fair.

PAULA. Because I'm going to make the sale, and I'm going to make it for both of you. You're going to get 50 percent each. All three of us, plus Presley, are going to pose for the newspaper. I want to thank you both for fighting over him, thank you both for being winners, thank you for all the great sales advice. And now I want you both, to sit back, and watch me sell Mr. Elvis Presley...car number 100.

*(**PAULA** moves toward exit.)*

Wish me luck, girls!

MONA. Good luck, Paula.

LORA. Good luck, Paula.

(**PAULA** *exits as both watch out to the showroom.*)

LORA. I can't believe it.

MONA. I can't either.

(pause)

LORA. Congratulations though.

MONA. Congratulations to you too.

(pause)

LORA. And I'm sorry.

MONA. I'm sorry too.

(pause)

BOTH TOGETHER TO THEMSELVES. You Loser!

(Lights fade. Blackout.)

INTRO TO SCENE SEVEN: "ONE PRIVATE GUARD"

(Lights fade in theatre, the following is heard:)

RADIO VOICE. *(serious tone)* Brace yourself Ladies and Gentlemen, *(pause)* this just in from Memphis, Tennessee,...

(pause) Elvis Presley, 42 years of age, the "King of Rock n' Roll," has died!

(trailing off) ...

(Pause. Lights up on Scene Six.)

ONE PRIVATE GUARD

SET

Bare stage

TIME

August, 1977

PLACE

Tupelo, Mississippi

CAST

Guard

ONE PRIVATE GUARD was first produced by the Metropolitan Theatre Company in New York City as a selection of the Midtown International Theatre Festival, at the Where Eagles Dare Theatre, 347 West 36th Street, on July 18, 2007. Executive producer, John Chatterton; managing director, Emileena Pedigo; artistic director, Glory Sims Bowen; marketing director, Bob Ost. The play was directed by Branan Whitehead; stage managed by Lloyd Fass; produced by Luigi Jannuzzi/Branan Whitehead; lighting and sound design by Lloyd Fass and Branan Whitehead. The cast was as follows:

GUARD *(Male or Female)* . . . . CRAIG CLARY

(Lights rise on one **GUARD**.*)*

GUARD. Sir, the entrance to Graceland is around the corner. And if you are leaving condolences about the death of Mr. Presley last week...Mrs. Presley would like to ask for your patience in receiving a thank you note, since she has been overwhelmed with flowers and cards.

(pause)

Me?

(pause)

Oh, all right. Ask away. And what newspaper would that be?

(pause)

Oh I get that paper, everyone in town gets that.

(pause)

Well, I'm flattered. And willing to answer anything you want. But I gotta tell ya, if this story you're writing is trying to dig up dirt, I'm going to disappoint you. I have nothing but positive things to say about Mr. Presley.

(pause)

Uh...ten years.

(pause)

Mostly customer service. But in the last week we've just needed more people outside to talk to people.

(pause)

Yes, I have. I've traveled three times with him: Once to Hawaii, at the Block Arena at Pearl Harbor, when he donated all the proceeded to complete the U.S.S. Arizona Memorial. Remember, they ran out of money. But then, after that, they completed it the next year.

(pause)

And I traveled with him to buy the former presidential yacht of Franklin Delano Roosevelt's. I think it was named 'The Potomac.' I know a lot about boats, raised on them, that's why he took me. He bought the yacht, gave it to Danny Thomas for underprivileged children at Saint Jude's Hospital. That was a great boat, great gesture. I was there.

(pause)

And the last time was when Mr. Presley donated all that money, I think it's still the largest amount ever donated by an individual to the Actor's Fund...what was it,...the Motion Picture Relief fund. He took me cause he knew I love Barbara Stanwyck. Miss Stanwyck and Mr. Sinatra accepted the gift for the Actors. See this is not interesting. This in not what you want. You want me to tell you dirt and some taboo secrets but I don't have any.

(pause)

Whoops. And my shifts over.

(pause)

Yup, that's my name, exactly how it's spelt on my name tag. And I gotta go, my husband's gotta dentist appointment and I'm a little short on time. But I'll tell you what you do, come back tomorrow. Same door just about five hours earlier. And I'll talk till you run out of ink. Okay?

(pause)

Well, okay then. And I'm very honored that your paper would do a story on just a service rep here. So...I'll see you tomorrow.

(GUARD *waves, exits.)*

(blackout)

INTRO TO SCENE EIGHT: "LEAVING GRACELAND"

(Lights fade in theatre, the following is heard.)

RADIO VOICE. In the news today...

> *(Please insert something here that happened today. Make it about three sentences, nothing depressing or shocking. Mention the current President, Governor or a popular sports or news story so everyone will realize that it is today's news.)*
>
> *(Be careful to not slander anyone or state anything that is not in a newspaper or heard from a reliable radio or television station.)*
>
> *(trailing off) ...*
>
> *(Pause. Lights up on Scene Eight.)*

LEAVING GRACELAND

SET
Bare stage

TIME
Now

PLACE
Graceland, Memphis, Tennessee

CAST
Eddie

Leslie

On or Offstage Voice or Voices

LEAVING GRACELAND was first produced by the Metropolitan Theatre Company in New York City as a selection of the Midtown International Theatre Festival, at the Where Eagles Dare Theatre, 347 West 36th Street, on July 18, 2007. Executive producer, John Chatterton; managing director, Emileena Pedigo; artistic director, Glory Sims Bowen; marketing director, Bob Ost. The play was directed by Branan Whitehead; stage managed by Lloyd Fass; produced by Luigi Jannuzzi/Branan Whitehead; lighting and sound design by Lloyd Fass and Branan Whitehead. The cast was as follows:

EDDIE . . . . CRAIG CLARY
LESLIE . . . . JESSICA ASCH*
ON OR OFFSTAGE VOICE or **VOICES** . . . . REBECCA BATEMAN
ALISHA CAMPBELL

*Also appeared as **LESLIE** . . . . JENNIFER BELVINS

(Lights rise on **EDDIE** *and* **LESLIE.** *on bare stage.)*

*(***EDDIE** *is in jeans and shirt and should not be dressed as an impersonator.)*

EDDIE. You can't Leslie.

LESLIE. I gotta.

EDDIE. You can't leave, Leslie.

LESLIE. I am leaving.

OFFSTAGE VOICE. Leslie?

LESLIE. What?

OFFSTAGE VOICE. Where are the silhouette salt and pepper shakers?

LESLIE. 2nd closet, 2 shelf on the left, right behind the 16 piece dinnerware set.

OFFSTAGE VOICE. Thanks.

EDDIE. Leslie, you can't leave me floating out here alone.

LESLIE. I'm sorry.

EDDIE. Look at me. I'm rising. I'm number three now.

LESLIE. Ten years, four spots.

EDDIE. I was number eight, now three. That's five spots Leslie. I have bounded five spots to the almost two, then one position.

LESLIE. But what is "one," it's still an impersonator.

EDDIE. Don't use that word. I told you never use that word, the only people who use that word do not know the business.

LESLIE. That's the word though.

EDDIE. I am a messenger of the King. I am fulfilling Mr Presley's wishes of having his songs performed, in his town, to his people, with the artistic honesty and purity to which he has set down in his musical diaries.

LESLIE. Oh my God, I am getting memorized responses. This is the lowest form of communication.

OFFSTAGE VOICE. Leslie?

LESLIE. What?

OFFSTAGE VOICE. Ralph can't find the Presley Place Teddy Bears.

LESLIE. We moved all bears to first closet on left. First shelf is Presley Place, second is "Musical Teddy," third is the "Musical Teddy" with the "I Love Elvis" sweater.

EDDIE. Leslie, you knew that was going to be my response, it's the plaque in the dressing room we all hit on the way out.

LESLIE. Oh, by the way, I not only quit as a back up singer, I also just quit the souvenir shop.

EDDIE. *(gasps)*

LESLIE. Just now.

EDDIE. No.

LESLIE. Go ask.

EDDIE. You can't.

LESLIE. I can, I did and so can you. Hang up the jumpsuit, the big belt, the fake sideburns and walk.

EDDIE. I could never.

LESLIE. I'm walking to the community college tomorrow and I'm registering.

EDDIE. For what?

LESLIE. A college degree.

EDDIE. In what?

LESLIE. Not sure, but I'm getting one 'cause you can get a higher paying job with one and that's what I want.

OFFSTAGE VOICE. Leslie?

LESLIE. I quit!

OFFSTAGE VOICE. One more?

LESLIE. What?

OFFSTAGE VOICE. The Elvis mouse pads.

LESLIE. Which ones?

OFFSTAGE VOICE. There's two right?

LESLIE. Three. Second closet 1st shelf. One: there's the Elvis plain one's, two: the screen saver and mouse, and three: there's the ever popular 68 comeback special pad. They're all next to the virtual Graceland CD roms.

OFFSTAGE VOICE. Okay.

EDDIE. How tall are the salt and pepper shakers?

LESLIE. Three and a half inches tall, times one and a quarter inch in diameter. they're pretty nice, bought some for my Mom, real durable, made of plastic and metal, they bounce.

EDDIE. Wow! I didn't know you had them.

LESLIE. I am telling you that I have quit both of my jobs and you're thinking about salt and pepper shakers?

EDDIE. How long have you had them?

LESLIE. *(pause)* They're a big seller, Eddie.

(lively, like a salesperson)

And they come complete with a musical note plastic base for easy storage and carrying. Made in China.

EDDIE. Before you leave, could you get me one with your discount?

LESLIE. No.

EDDIE. Come on.

LESLIE. Absolutely not!

EDDIE. Please?

LESLIE. And this is why the other night I was questioning whether we should even be dating.

EDDIE. Leslie, I don't think we should talk about that now.

LESLIE. And you couldn't understand why? This is "why." Look at you, you're obsessing on Elvis memorabilia and I am LEAVING EVERYTHING!

OFFSTAGE VOICE. Leslie?

EDDIE. I'm sorry, Leslie.

OFFSTAGE VOICE. I'm sorry, Leslie, but Ralph is crazy, we're swamped…and some guy wants fifty three glasses with the high, uh…what do you call it?

LESLIE. Stem. The word is "stem." We have two: One, the stemmed goblet set that says, "Elvis Presley's Heartbreak Hotel." Or the martini glass set that also says, "Elvis Presley's Heartbreak Hotel."

OFFSTAGE VOICE. What's the difference?

LESLIE. The martini glass is shallow, more of a V. The goblet is a water goblet. First closet, third shelf on top. Be careful the ladder wobbles.

OFFSTAGE VOICE. Thanks. And Ralph says, if you'll come back, he'll pay you double time just for today.

LESLIE. I quit! Doesn't anybody around here understand. I'm waiting for my ride and I'm gone.

EDDIE. Okay, so you're going to college and you're getting...uh.

LESLIE. Out of here! That's where I'm getting, "Out of here." This is not reality, Eddie. This is a time warp. It's like a fifties tar pit that everyone's stuck in. It's like some religious cult where the leader's quit cause he doesn't even want to be a part of it anymore but people join just to make believe they could have believed. It's so weird.

EDDIE. He didn't quit. He had an unfortunate happening.

LESLIE. Eddie, about a week ago I had a dream that Elvis came into the shop. And he kissed me. And he thanked me. And then he picked me up and put me on the shelf right next to you. And we were souvenirs for him. And everyone that worked here was across from us on another shelf and it was so frightening cause everyone was frozen. Even me, cause we didn't want to move, we were so in awe. *(pause)* I don't want to be a souvenir, Eddie. Time warps when I wasn't alive, don't interest me. I still have one foot out of the tar pit and I'm pullin' out. And my advice to you would be, come with me.

EDDIE. No.

LESLIE. Enroll in the music program at the college. They have a lot of courses. I brought a catalogue home for you.

EDDIE. Leslie, tell me that we can still date?

LESLIE. Eddie, we can still date.

EDDIE. Whoa...I was scared there.

LESLIE. But I have three rules.

OFFSTAGE VOICE. Leslie?

LESLIE. What?

OFFSTAGE VOICE. One last?

LESLIE. What is it?

OFFSTAGE VOICE. King's Blend Coffee? Do we sell by the brick?

LESLIE. No. We sell by the set. A set is three vacuum packed bricks of Arabian gourmet coffee, two ounces each. Don't break up the sets.

OFFSTAGE VOICE. And we need one cue ball?

LESLIE. Closet three, second shelf. The Elvis cue ball sets are between the "Barbie loves Elvis gift sets" and the "Elvis, The Army Years" dolls.

EDDIE. Barbie huh? I wonder how Prisilla feels about that?

LESLIE. One: I'm not coming to see you do Elvis impersonations anymore.

EDDIE. Okay.

LESLIE. Two: We're not going to see *anyone* do Elvis impersonations anymore.

EDDIE. How about if.

LESLIE. No one!

EDDIE. Okay.

LESLIE. And three: We are not going to see any more Elvis movies.

EDDIE. Then what are we going to do?

LESLIE. Well for a start, we could see any other movie made.

EDDIE. Well.

LESLIE. See...you have no concept of anything that does not include Elvis, do you? You cannot even entertain the idea, can you? And it's sad, Eddie. It's worst than sad, it's...really...really...sad. It's frightening. Years, seasons are changing, Eddie, and you're focusing on your sideburns.

EDDIE. So we won't see each other everyday?

LESLIE. I'm sorry.

EDDIE. And we won't have lunch together?

LESLIE. No we won't.

EDDIE. And I won't be giving you a ride home?

LESLIE. You can come over after work. Hey there's my Mom.

OFFSTAGE VOICE. Leslie?

LESLIE. No more.

OFFSTAGE VOICE. Leslie, please?

LESLIE. I refuse to answer any more questions on the inner chambers of the Graceland souvenir closets.

OFFSTAGE VOICE. Ralph is ripping one of the closets apart.

LESLIE. That's one way to learn.

OFFSTAGE VOICE. He can't find the "Jailhouse Rock Magnetic Clock." We found "The Blinking Lights Alarm Clock," "The Retro Alarm Clock" and "The Swinging Elvis Motion Clock, but where's the "Jailhouse Rock Magnetic Clock," Leslie. For the love of God, please tell me? He's going to hurt himself then I'll be in charge and I don't know where anything is!

LESLIE. The answer is: There are none! *(pause)* And like me: We're out! We're finally out! They're gone! Fini.

OFFSTAGE VOICE. Thanks Leslie. We didn't even think of that.

LESLIE. My Mom's waiting, Eddie. I gotta go.

EDDIE. Can I see you tonight, Leslie?

LESLIE. How about tomorrow night, Eddie. Tonight I just want to sit home and…sit home.

EDDIE. Tomorrow night.

LESLIE. At six.

EDDIE. At six.

LESLIE. Bring a video, we'll watch it.

EDDIE. On what?

LESLIE. Anything but.

EDDIE. I know.

(LESLIE moves up to EDDIE.)

LESLIE. Don't feel so bad, Eddie. It's going to be okay.

EDDIE. I feel like Elvis died again.

LESLIE. What are you talking about, Eddie? You weren't even alive when Elvis died.

EDDIE. But this is probably what it felt like. It's very sad.

LESLIE. You think that's sad? I'll tell you what's sad. They don't know they're nearly out of the Elvis Pink Cadillac Die Cast Car, the T.V. Cookie Jar, or down to their last box of the biggest seller of all, in there, the 24 by 5 inch metal "Lonely Street, Memphis, Tennessee" signs.

EDDIE. *(Gasps.)* You're not going to tell them?

LESLIE. I'll sleep on it.

(LESLIE moves toward exit.)

Cause you know when they run out,...there's going to be,...a "whole lotta shakin' going on!"

(LESLIE laughs. Exits.)

(EDDIE laughs, stops, pauses, looks toward souvenir place, pauses, toward where Leslie exited, pauses, back at souvenir place, pauses, back toward where Leslie exited.)

EDDIE. *(yells)* Leslie?

LESLIE. *(offstage.)* What?

EDDIE. Can I come over *tonight* to look at the college catalogue, Leslie?

(EDDIE exits, running toward LESLIE.)

(Blackout. End of Play.)

Breinigsville, PA USA
16 December 2010
251635BV00005B/14/P